GREEN LIZARDS AND RED RECTANGLES AND the Blue Ball

Steve Antony

The **GREEN LIZARDS** and the
RED RECTANGLES lived peacefully together.

Until . . .

the **Blue Ball** came along.

The **LIZARDS** and the **RECTANGLES** had never seen a **Ball** before.

So they built a WALL to keep it out.

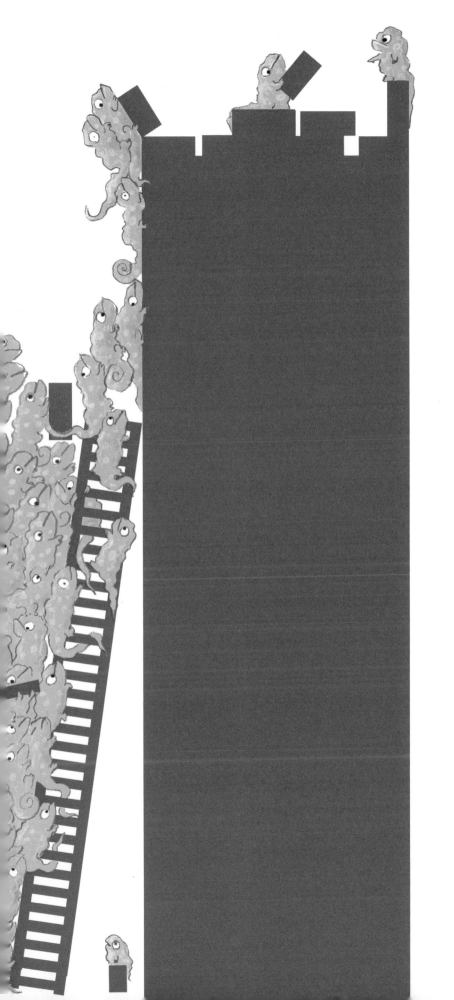

The Blue Ball
was all alone.

Then one day . . .

the WALL.

climbed over

and a little **RED RECTANGLE**

a little **GREEN LIZARD**

Do you want to play?

So beyond the wall they played...

and played... and played... and played...

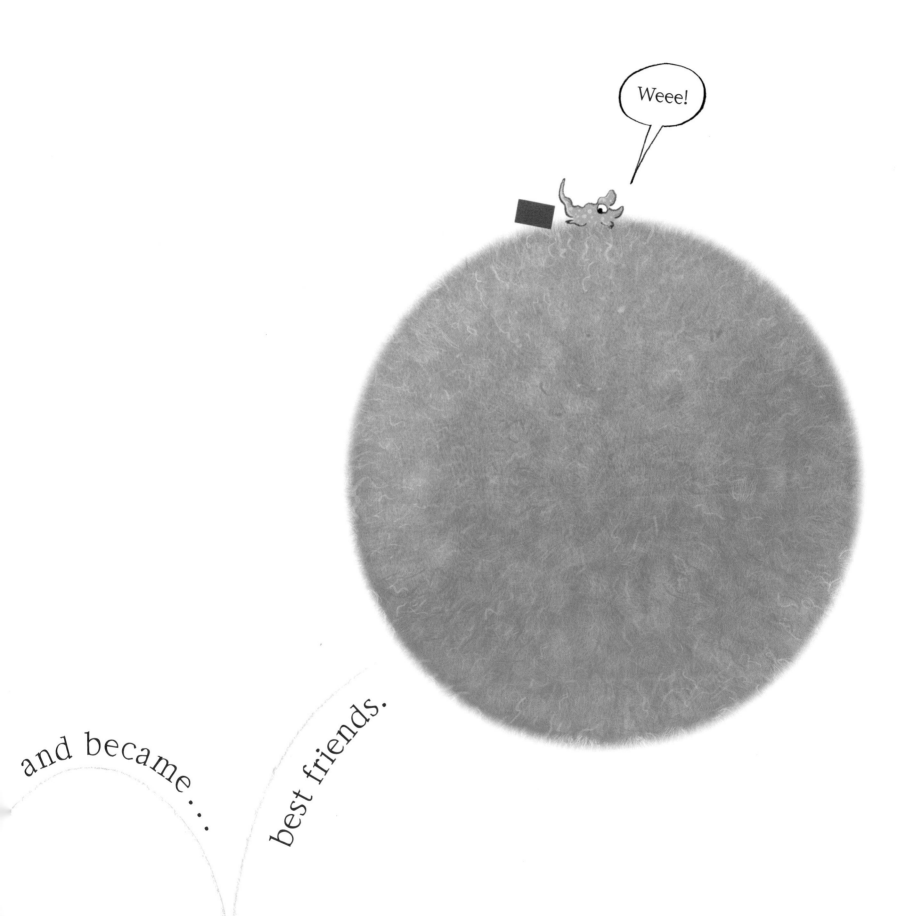

Some of the
GREEN LIZARDS
and **RED RECTANGLES**
didn't like this.

YOU CAN'T BE FRIENDS WITH THE Blue Ball!

But others ...

wanted to play too!

It wasn't long before . . .

EVERYONE

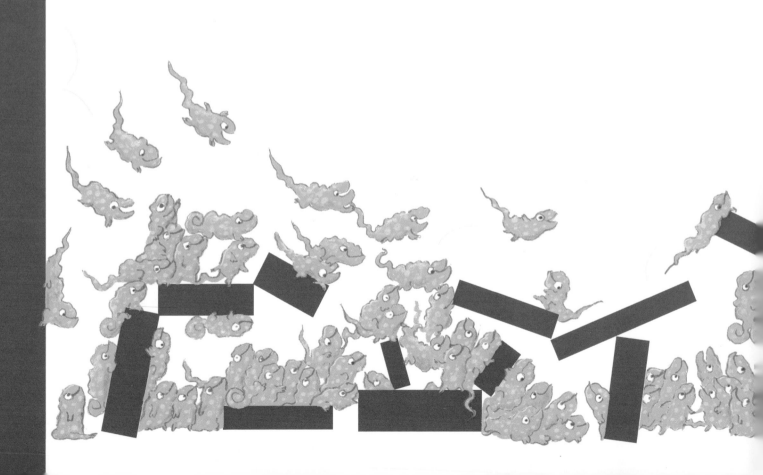

joined in the fun!

The wall that once divided them . . .

SMASH

ED and came tumbling down.

Once more, the **GREEN LIZARDS** and the **RED RECTANGLES** lived peacefully together...

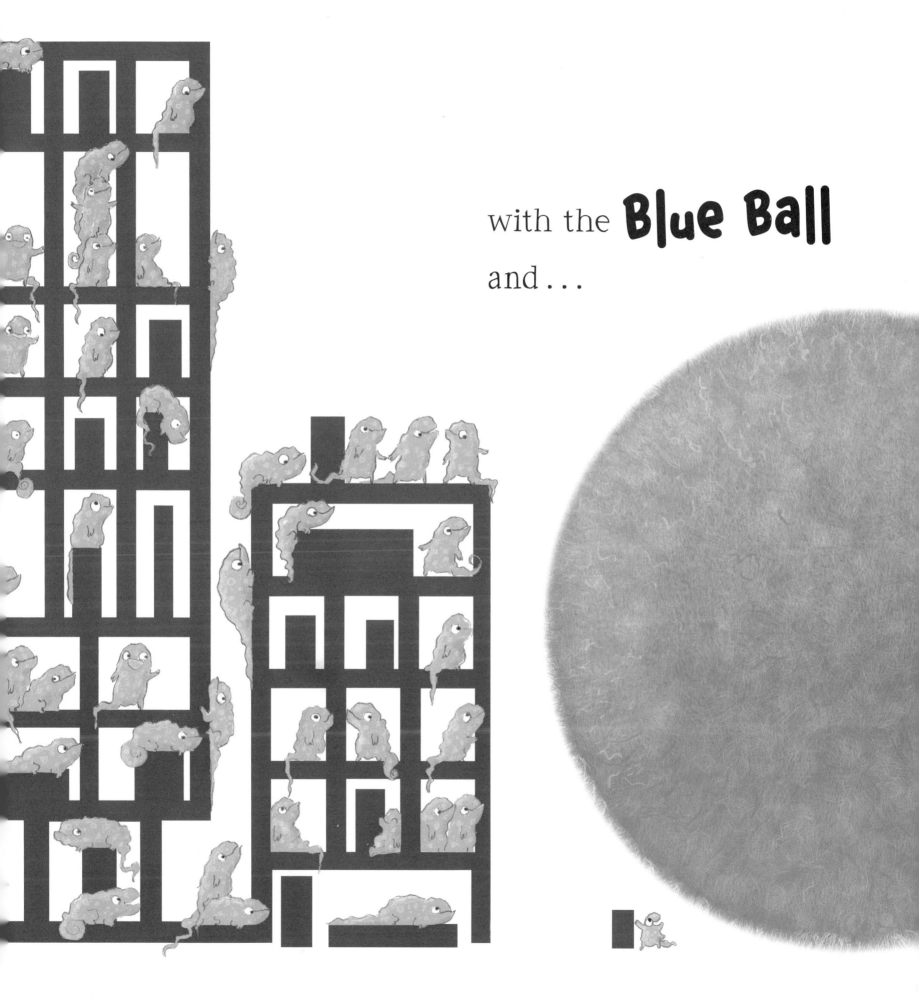

with the **Blue Ball** and . . .

every

shape, size and colour.